W9-CHW-005

Grumpy Bear

Best Friend Bear

Secret Bear

This book belongs to:

Fischer

Wish Bear

Love-a-lot Bear

Care Bears™ © 2006 Those Characters From Cleveland, Inc.
Used under license by Scholastic Inc. All rights reserved.

No part of this publication may be reproduced in whole or in part, or stored in a retrieval system,
or transmitted in any form or by any means, electronic, mechanical, photocopying, recording, or
otherwise, without written permission of the publisher. For information regarding permission,
write to: Scholastic Inc., Attention: Permissions Department, 557 Broadway, New York, NY 10012.

Published by Scholastic Inc.
90 Old Sherman Turnpike, Danbury, CT 06816.

SCHOLASTIC and associated logos are trademarks and/or registered trademarks of Scholastic Inc.

ISBN 0-439-83581-X

First Scholastic Printing, April 2006

Care Bears™
Friendship Club

Secret Surprise!

by
Quinlan B. Lee

Illustrated by
Saxton Moore

SCHOLASTIC INC.

New York   Toronto   London   Auckland   Sydney
Mexico City   New Delhi   Hong Kong   Buenos Aires

It was the day before Secret Bear's birthday.
She and Wish Bear were playing a cloud game.

"That one looks like a star," said Wish Bear.
"It's perfect for wishing."

"And that one looks like a big balloon," said
Secret Bear. "I love balloons. Don't you, Wish Bear?"

Wish Bear shook her head. "Can you keep **a secret?**" she asked. "I'm afraid of balloons."

"You are?" Secret Bear said gently.
"Why?"

"They scare me when they pop,"
Wish Bear replied. "Isn't that silly?"
"Not at all," said Secret Bear.
"Loud noises can be scary sometimes."

9

Wish Bear knew her secret would be safe
with Secret Bear. Wish Bear also knew the best
way to celebrate

Secret Bear's Birthday.

"If only the Care Bears can keep the surprise **a secret!**" Wish Bear thought.

Secret Bear's birthday finally arrived.
Secret Bear found Best Friend Bear
picking flowers.

"Oh my!"
Best Friend Bear cried.

"I'm sorry," said Secret Bear. "Did I startle you?"

"Um . . . no," Best Friend Bear mumbled. "I just didn't want you to find my secret flower patch."

"I won't tell," Secret Bear promised her.

Share Bear was busy baking. "Secret Bear! What are *you* doing here?" Share Bear asked.

"Nothing much," Secret Bear replied.

"Is something wrong?"

"N . . . no,"
Share Bear stammered.
"I . . . um . . . I just didn't
want to share the
secret ingredient
in my sprinkle
cupcakes."

When Secret Bear saw Love-a-lot Bear
and Funshine Bear filling up balloons, they hid
behind a cloud.

Secret Bear was confused. Why were all her
friends acting so strangely? Not a single one of them
had even wished her a happy birthday!

Then Secret Bear saw Bedtime Bear and Grumpy Bear. They quickly covered up the big sign they were painting.

"It's for our secret club," they told her.

"Oh," Secret Bear replied sadly.
"I'll leave you alone."

19

"You look like you could use some cheering up," Cheer Bear said when she saw Secret Bear's sad face. "No one wants to tell me their secrets anymore," said Secret Bear. "I don't understand why.

I always keep secrets safe."

"We know that," said Cheer Bear.
"But sometimes we have to keep
something secret until it's just
the right time to share it."

"I know! Let's go visit Share Bear.
Follow me!" said Cheer Bear.

Care-a-lot Castle was quiet . . .
until suddenly all the Care Bears
jumped out and shouted,

"Surprise!"

"Happy Secret Surprise Birthday!" added Wish Bear.

Y BIRTHDAY secret Bear!

Secret Bear laughed.
"You all can keep a secret
even better than me!"

The Care Bears sang and danced and played games.

Soon it was time
for presents.

Funshine Bear
and Love-a-lot Bear
gave Secret Bear a
special surprise—a big
bunch of balloons.

"Time to share the cake," said Share Bear.
"Let's sing, and then Secret Bear can make her **wish**."

"Wait," said Cheer Bear, looking around. "Where's Wish Bear? Secret Bear can't make a wish without Wish Bear."

"I think I know," said Secret Bear.

Wish Bear was hiding behind a star.
"The balloons scared me," she told Secret
Bear. "Did you tell everyone I'm a
scaredy-bear?"

"Of course not," said Secret Bear.

"Friends keep each other's secrets locked in their hearts."

31

Wish Bear gave Secret Bear a big hug. "Thanks for keeping my secret."

"That's what I'm here for," said Secret Bear. "And now I need your help. It's time for me to make my birthday wish."

"And that's what *I'm* here for," Wish Bear said happily.

Secret Bear took a big breath and blew out her candle. "I wished everyone could have as great a birthday as mine," she said.

"You are the **beary best** friends a Care Bear could have," said Secret Bear.

"That wish will surely come true!" said Wish Bear.

Can You Keep a Secret Like Secret Bear?

Wish Bear doesn't want anyone else to know
her secret. She only tells Secret Bear.

❤ Have you ever told a friend a secret?

❤ Did your friend keep it safe?

Secret Bear kept Wish Bear's secret locked in her heart.

❤ What do you think would have happened if Secret Bear had told the other Care Bears?

❤ How would Wish Bear have felt?

Some secrets, like the surprise party, you have to keep only for a little while.

❤ Can you think of a secret like that?

❤ Are secrets hard or easy for you to keep?

Bashful Heart Bear

Cheer Bear

Share Bear

Bedtime Bear

Funshine Bear